Aliens from outer space are threatening to invade Earth, and everyone looks to Superman for help. But this time, something goes wrong, and Superman is defeated. If the Man of Steel cannot save Earth, what is going to happen?

British Library Cataloguing in Publication Data

Levin, David
    Double trouble.
    I. Title   II. Davies, Robin, *1950-*
813'.54 [J]
    ISBN 0-7214-1180-0

First edition

Published by Ladybird Books Ltd Loughborough Leicestershire UK
Ladybird Books Inc Auburn Maine 04210 USA

Printed in England

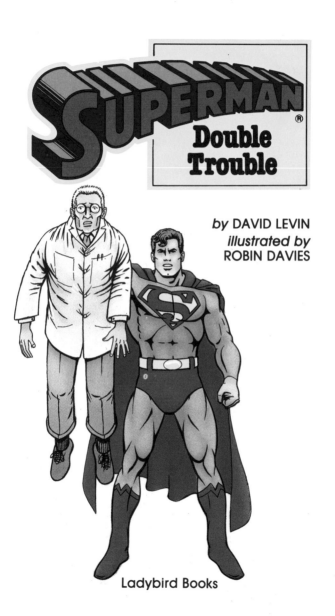

SUPERMAN ®
Double Trouble

by DAVID LEVIN
illustrated by
ROBIN DAVIES

Ladybird Books

One Tuesday afternoon in mid-July, reporters and photographers crowded to the windows of the *Daily Planet* to look up at the sky.

Five strange ships floated overhead – four small round "flying saucers", and a larger one, a mother ship. They made no sound as they hovered, giving no clue at all as to what they were, where they came from, or what they wanted.

Down below, Lois Lane and Jimmy
Olsen strolled out of the *Daily Planet*
building on their way to lunch. They'd
been in the lift, and hadn't heard the
excitement.

As they went into the street, however,
Jimmy stopped in his tracks. "Wow! Look
at *that*!" he said, pointing.

"What a story!" cried Lois, as she
looked up at the five ships.

As she spoke, the ships suddenly started moving again, and a few minutes later they came to rest above the Qurac Consulate. Lois and Jimmy moved fast, but by the time they reached the spot, the police were there too.

Lois's old friend, Police Inspector Bill Henderson, was standing at the entrance.

"What do these flying saucers want, Bill?" asked Lois.

"I wish I knew," he replied. "I must admit I'd feel a lot better if Superman would show up!"

Just then, a strange metallic voice came from the mother ship with a message of pure evil. "Attention, people of Earth! We are invaders from the planet Lorsendia! Your world has just 24 hours to surrender to us or die!"

Then the alien ships began to shoot laser beams at the city below. As people ran for cover, the question on everyone's lips was, "Why isn't Superman here?"

Lois and Jimmy raced back to the *Daily Planet*, where their boss Perry White had stopped the presses for their report.

In the White House in Washington, the President picked up his phone. "These aliens must be stopped!" he said firmly. "If Superman can't help, we shall have to do it ourselves!"

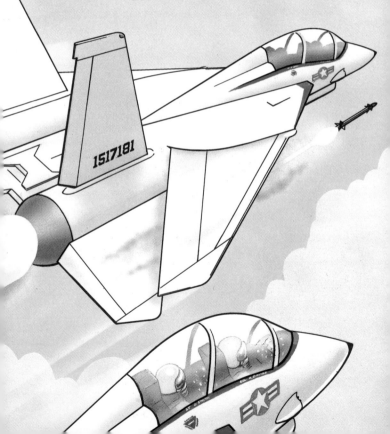

Minutes later, fighter jets began to take off for Metropolis. As soon as the pilots reached the alien ships, they began firing. But a protective force field round the strange ships kept the missiles from finding their targets!

"Foolish Earthlings, you cannot defeat us!" boomed the voice from the mother ship. "Our advanced technology keeps us from harm. Now you have only 20 hours to surrender!"

And once more people began to ask, "Where is Superman?"

Next morning the flying saucers were still above the city. Inside the United Nations, members were discussing the best way to deal with the alien invasion.

Lois and Jimmy were outside the *Planet* building, waiting for something new to happen, when suddenly they saw a familiar flash of red, yellow and blue!

"Look!" yelled Jimmy. "It's Superman!"
The Man of Steel lifted one of the ships high above his head, preparing to hurl it

back into space. Suddenly, the alien voice spoke again. "Stop, Superman! Do not attempt to harm our ship!"

"You leave me no choice," said the hero. "You have attacked my planet!"

At that moment, the doors of the mother ship opened, and the voice said, "Enter, Superman, and you will see why we cannot be defeated!"

Superman flew straight inside, and the doors slid shut behind him.

The crowd below waited anxiously, Lois and Jimmy amongst them. When the figure of Superman at last flew out and down, everyone cheered.

News reporters and television cameras swarmed around their hero as he landed. Superman looked down at the ground as he spoke. "My friends... for years, I have protected you from every danger. But now, I cannot help.

"These aliens are too powerful for us! We must surrender to them at once, or we will all die!" he finished unhappily. With that, Superman flew off into the sky, and disappeared.

Back in the *Daily Planet* offices, Lois said to her editor, "I just can't believe that Superman would give up like that."

"If *he* can't defeat the invaders, what chance do the rest of us have? It looks as though they've won," said Perry White.

But in the penthouse of the mighty Lexcorp Building, one man in Metropolis was not unhappy. A smile danced across Lex Luthor's face as he thought, "At last the world has seen Superman for the paper hero he really is! My plan has worked."

He lifted the phone to speak to his secret laboratory, somewhere in Metropolis. "Doctor Howitzer," he said, "how goes it?"

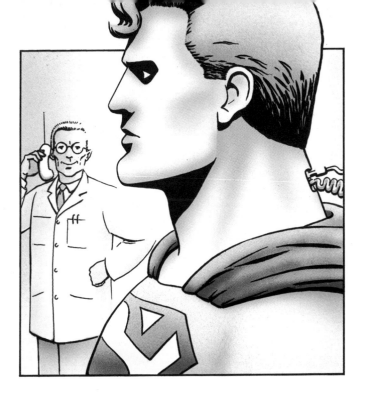

Howitzer was Luthor's chief scientist and engineer. "It has all gone perfectly," he said. "But best of all has been the double!" He looked across at a figure standing stiffly in the corner of his lab. It was the figure of Superman.

"Ah yes, your Superman robot!" said Luthor. "Now that we've destroyed Superman's reputation, we will soon control the world as well!"

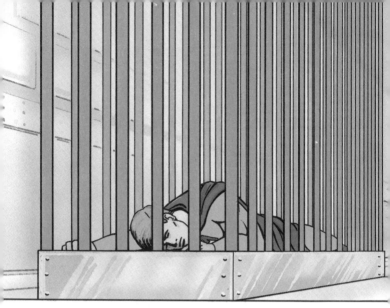

Howitzer smiled. He touched a button on his desk and a cage began to rise up from the floor, its bars glowing green. Inside the cage, the *real* Superman lay slumped on the floor. Kryptonite radiation flowing through the steel bars of the cage was sapping his strength.

"You and Luthor will never get away with this evil plan!" said Superman weakly, looking across at Howitzer.

From the other end of the phone, Luthor heard Superman's voice and laughed. "We've already got away with it, Superman!" His two-fold plan was

working perfectly! Superman was completely trapped as long as the cage's Kryptonite rays were activated, and the bogus flying saucer invaders that Howitzer had designed had already terrified people everywhere.

Now that the world knew that Superman could not help, it would soon surrender.

Howitzer grinned as he put the phone down. Then he went back to his latest project, a giant magnifying lens, and ignored Superman in his cage.

When Luthor put down his phone, he turned to look at a bank of television screens opposite him. On them, the United Nations members were still discussing whether to surrender or not.

Most countries were in favour of it, but some were still holding out. Luthor grinned to himself as he watched.

Back in Howitzer's laboratories, Superman was growing weaker by the minute as the Kryptonite radiation poured into his cage. Then he got an idea. Using all his concentration, the Man of Steel aimed his weakened heat vision ray into the lens Howitzer was working on.

The giant lens magnified and strengthened the ray. The ray bent as it went through the glass, and hit the control panel, which began to glow from the heat. Howitzer had his back towards Superman, and he'd forgotten all about his prisoner. The Man of Steel hoped he wouldn't notice. Just...a...few...more... seconds...and...

KAPOW! The control panel exploded as it overheated and the cage was shattered by the flying metal. The Kryptonite radiation stopped in an instant. Howitzer turned in shock and backed away as Superman jumped up.

"And now..." said Superman starting forward. Then the Man of Steel paused. His super-hearing had picked up the screams of helpless people.

"Great Krypton!" he shouted. "When I smashed the control panel, it must have set off the lasers in the UFOs!"

And he was right – the fake UFOs were now shooting lasers all over Metropolis! First of all, Superman tied up the scientist, saying, "You'll stay put there for now! I must stop those lasers!"

With that, he left, flying at top speed to the Qurac Consulate. There the laser beams from the sky were demolishing and destroying buildings one by one.

The terrified people of Metropolis crept back to watch Superman as he flew into the largest UFO, smashing it to smithereens! "One down, four to go!" he shouted triumphantly.

"Look!" said Lois. "Superman has destroyed the largest space ship! I knew he couldn't really have given up!"

Meanwhile, Lex Luthor hit a remote control button that started up his robot Superman in the secret lab. He barked his orders, "Get rid of Superman! Destroy him!"

The robot sprang to life. Reaching Superman just as he was smashing apart the second UFO, the robot double crashed into him, throwing him into the river.

"Get that on film!" Lois cried out to Jimmy as *two* Supermen flew into the air and launched into battle high above Metropolis. While they fought, the other "flying saucers" continued to fire lasers at the streets below!

As the battle raged to and fro, the watching crowd realised the truth. "Those ships weren't alien! Superman never surrendered at all. It must have been that impostor who's fighting him now."

High above them, Superman grabbed the robot double and hurled him into one of the alien ships. The ship exploded into a thousand pieces over the river – and so did the robot version of Superman!

"Wow!" exclaimed Jimmy. "The phoney Superman was a robot!"

Finally, with the robot and the third ship destroyed, Superman crashed the other two alien ships together.

The invasion was over and everyone realised that Superman had *not* let them down. He was their hero once more.

Superman flew to Luthor's office, taking the scientist, Howitzer, with him. "Luthor!" he shouted. "Your scientist is going to jail. And I won't rest until the day I can put *you* there as well."

Luthor shrugged. "No chance, Superman. Howitzer's got nothing to do with me. I fired him last year," he said calmly.

Later, in the *Daily Planet* offices, Lois Lane typed up the true story of Superman's struggle against the saucers. Just then, Clark Kent walked into the room. "Clark! Where have you been?"

"Me, Lois? I was just covering the story from a different angle," he said, with a grin.

Things were back to normal again.